JON SCIESZKA'S TRUCKTOWN

KAT'S MAPS

BY JON SCIESZKA

CHARACTERS AND ENVIRONMENTS DEVELOPED BY THE

dESIGN garage

DAVID SHANNON   **LOREN LONG**   **DAVID GORDON**

ILLUSTRATION CREW:

Executive Producer:

TOT
INDUSTRIES

Creative Supervisor: Nina Rappaport Brown ○ Drawings by: Dan Root ○ Color by: Antonio Reyna

Art Director: Laura Roode

Ready-to-Read

Simon Spotlight

New York   London   Toronto   Sydney

SIMON SPOTLIGHT
An imprint of Simon & Schuster Children's Publishing Division
1230 Avenue of the Americas, New York, NY 10020
Copyright © 2011 by JRS Worldwide, LLC.
TRUCKTOWN and JON SCIESZKA'S TRUCKTOWN and design are trademarks
of JRS Worldwide, LLC. All rights reserved, including the right of reproduction in
whole or in part in any form. SIMON SPOTLIGHT, READY-TO-READ, and colophon
are registered trademarks of Simon & Schuster, Inc.
For information about special discounts for bulk purchases, please contact Simon &
Schuster Special Sales at 1-866-506-1949 or business@simonandschuster.com.
Manufactured in the United States of America 0511 LAK
First Simon Spotlight edition, June 2011
10 9 8 7 6 5 4 3 2 1
Library of Congress Cataloging-in-Publication Data
Scieszka, Jon.
Kat's maps / by Jon Scieszka ; artwork created by The Design Garage: David Gordon,
Loren Long, David Shannon. — 1st Simon Spotlight ed.
p. cm. — (Jon Scieszka's Trucktown) (Ready-to-read)
Summary: Kat, who loves to make maps of all sorts of places and things, gives a special
map to Jack.
[1. Maps—Fiction. 2. Drawing—Fiction.] I. Design Garage. II. Title.
PZ7.S41267Kas 2011
[E]—dc22
2009046920
ISBN 978-1-4169-4148-4 (pbk)
ISBN 978-1-4169-4159-0 (hc)

Kat makes maps.

Kat makes maps
of her room,

[Kat's Ro

Lamp

Desk

Floor
Mat

maps of her block,

my house

flower box

N

maps of her town,

and maps of her world.

Kat loves maps.

Kat makes maps of her mind

and maps of her heart.

"Here is a map for you,"
says Kat to Jack.

"Where does it go?"

"To a surprise."

Jack follows Kat's map.

He turns left on
Motor Lane.

Jack drives over Speed Highway.

Under Race Bridge.

"An art show of all . . .

". . . Kat's maps."